Richard Scarry's
A Day at the
Airport

A Random House PICTUREBACK® Book

Random House ⌂ New York

Copyright © 2001 Richard Scarry Corporation. All rights reserved under International and Pan-American Copyright Conventions. Published in the United States by Random House, Inc., New York, and simultaneously in Canada by Random House of Canada Limited, Toronto. *Library of Congress Cataloging-in-Publication Data:* Scarry, Richard. [A Day at the airport] Richard Scarry's day at the airport. p.   cm. — (A pictureback book) SUMMARY: Rudolf Von Flugel takes Huckle, Sally, and Lowly on a tour of the airport. ISBN 0-375-81202-4 [1. Airports—Fiction.]   I. Title. II. Random House pictureback. PZ7.S327 Vi2001 [E]—dc21   00-044550

www.randomhouse.com/kids   Printed in the United States of America   April 2001   26 25 ˀ

Father Cat wants to take Huckle,
Sally, and Lowly out sailing this afternoon.
Plink! Plop! Plink!
Uh-oh, Father Cat, it's starting to rain.

"I guess that's the end of our sailing today!"
says Father Cat.

He puts the top up on the car.

"There's nothing to do but to go back home."

What a disappointment.

Father Cat stops at Scotty's Filling Station for gasoline.
"Fill 'er up, please, Scotty!" Father Cat says.
Just then, Rudolf Von Flugel drives up in his airplane-car.
"Good afternoon, Father Cat!" says Rudolf. "Are you going sailing?"

"No, we're going home, Rudolf," Father Cat says sadly. "The children will have to play inside today."

"Hmm," says Rudolf. "Why don't they come with me? I'm going to the airport. There's lots to see there, even when it rains!"

"Wow! Can we, Dad?" Huckle asks.

Father Cat thinks it is a great idea. He helps place the children in Rudolf's airplane-car.

"Don't worry, Father Cat. I'll bring the children home dry as baked apple strudel!" says Rudolf.

And off they go!
Brruumm!

runway

radar

pier

catering
truck

control
tower

snowplow

catering
kitchen

airport bus

They arrive at the airport in no time.

wind sock

runway lights

hangar

a tractor towing a plane

restaurant

departure terminal

parking garage

ARRIVALS DEPARTURES

arrivals

taxis

My, what a busy place it is!

check-in counters

TO PARIS ⬇

TO NEW YORK ⬇

TO VENICE ⬇

conveyor belt

scale

luggage cart

"Here we are!" Rudolf says, driving into the departure terminal.

TO THE GATES →

CLOSED ✗

TO WORKVILLE ↓

Mind your head!

luggage tag

DEPARTURES	TIME	GATE
PARIS	3:30	2
WORK VILLE	4:00	1
VENICE	4:02	3
NEW YORK	5:15	1
LONDON	5:30	3
TOKYO	6:00	2

lots of luggage

porter

"These are the check-in counters. Passengers show their tickets here, and also have their baggage weighed and tagged with its destination," Rudolf explains. "Each passenger receives a boarding pass to enter the plane at the gate."

check-in hostess

ticket

boarding pass

BOOKSHOP

POST OFFICE

TOILET

"The airport terminal is like a small Busytown," says Rudolf. "There are shops that sell books, toys, and flowers. And there's a police station, a post office, and a first-aid center, too!"

"Is there a bathroom, Mr. Von Flugel?" Sally asks.

BANANAS

CHAPEL

WATCHES

TOYS

FLOWERS

While they wait for Sally, Lowly asks if there is also a restaurant at the airport. "Travel always makes me thirsty!" he laughs.

As soon as Sally returns, Rudolf drives up the escalator to the restaurant.

RESTAURANT

restaurant

catering truck

boarding gate

WORKVILLE

passenger bus

kerosene fuel is pumped into tanks in the wings

baggage train

fire extinguisher

hose

cleaning truck

paper to recycle

bottles to recycle

"Wow! What a view!" exclaims Huckle.

electric generator

passenger bus

pier

plane positioner

waiting room

catering truck delivering meals

door

fuselage

cleaners cleaning the inside of the plane

tail

pilot and copilot

wing

baggage compartment

jet engine

baggage loader

baggage handler

flight crew arriving

ramp agent

tractor

Rudolf drives over to the control tower.
Please take care driving up the stairs, Rudolf.

catering kitchen
preparing meals

searchlight

radio antenna

runway

binoculars

ground controller

control tower

a taxiing plane heading for the runway

follow-me car guiding landed airplanes

FOLLOW ME

pilot studying the weather

weatherman

in winter, snowplows clear the runways and taxiways

"From up here, each plane receives instructions by radio—where to park and when to take off and land," Rudolf explains. "At night and in fog, you can still see every plane on this radar screen."

DON'T STEP ON THE GRASS.

radar antenna

radar screen

cargo plane

Just a little to the right!

"Ach! I almost forgot!" cries Rudolf.
He drives across the runway, past a
cargo plane being loaded with freight
containers.

airplane hangars

luggage
trolleys

freight
containers

"These are the hangars,
Sally," says Rudolf. "Inside,
airplanes are parked and
repaired."

"Thank you, Mr. Von Flugel,"
Sally replies. "But what's *that*!?"
she asks, pointing.

"Ach! *This* is my Bratwurst Balloon!" Rudolf says. "Quick! Hop in before you get wet!"

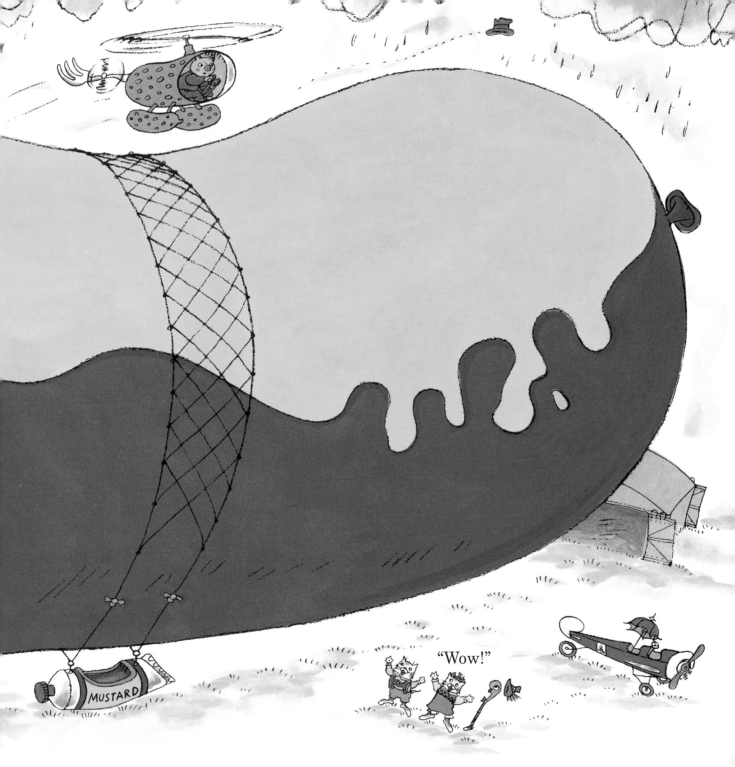

"Wow!"

"Look out, everyone!" calls the ground controller. "Here comes the Bratwurst Balloon!"

Soon they are high in the sky.

"Look! There's our house!" says Huckle.
"Mom! Dad! Look up!" he calls.

No, look *out,* Rudolf! Your Bratwurst Balloon is about to burst.

Bump! They all land safely on Huckle's front lawn.
"Well, Rudolf, that was a perfect landing," says Father Cat.
"Thank you, Mr. Von Flugel!" say Huckle, Sally, and Lowly.
"This has been the best afternoon ever!"